MINECRAFT
WITHER WITHOUT YOU
2

PRAISE FOR YOU, ME + ZOMBIES
YOU, ME + ZOMBIES
EYE OF THE TAIGA

MINECRAFT™

WITHER WITHOUT YOU

2

BY

KRISTEN GUDSNUK

COLOR ASSISTANT

NAKATA WHITTLE

DARK HORSE BOOKS

PRESIDENT & PUBLISHER
MIKE RICHARDSON

EDITOR
SHANTEL LaROCQUE

ASSOCIATE EDITOR
BRETT ISRAEL

DESIGNER
KEITH WOOD

DIGITAL ART TECHNICIANS
JOSIE CHRISTENSEN
AND **SAMANTHA HUMMER**

SPECIAL THANKS TO
JENNIFER HAMMERVALD, ALEX WILTSHIRE, KELSEY HOWARD,
AND **SHERIN KWAN**

Published by Dark Horse Books
A division of Dark Horse Comics LLC
10956 SE Main Street
Milwaukie, OR 97222

MINECRAFT.NET
DARKHORSE.COM
INTERNATIONAL LICENSING: 503-905-2377

To find a comics shop in your area, visit ComicShopLocator.com.

First edition: May 2021
Ebook ISBN 978-1-50671-889-7
Trade paperback ISBN 978-1-50671-886-6

10 9 8 7 6 5 4 3 2 1

Printed in China

Library of Congress Cataloging-in-Publication Data

Names: Gudsnuk, Kristen, artist, author.
Title: Minecraft : wither without you / by Kristen Gudsnuk.
Other titles: Wither without you
Description: First edition. | Milwaukie, OR : Dark Horse Books, 2020. | Series: Minecraft ; v. 1 | Audience: Ages 8+ | Summary: Cahira and Orion are twin monster hunters who go on a mission to get their mentor back, and meet Atria, a girl cursed as a monster lure, whom they convince to join their rescue mission to use her monster-attracting abilities to find the enchanted wither.
Identifiers: LCCN 2019053733 | ISBN 9781506708355 (trade paperback) | ISBN 9781506708645 (epub)
Subjects: LCSH: Graphic novels.
Classification: LCC PZ7.7.G83 Min 2020 | DDC 741.5/973--dc23
LC record available at https://lccn.loc.gov/2019053733

MINECRAFT™

IS THAT--?!
THE WITHER?!
KRAHH...
BUT HOW?!
UGGHHH.

HEY!
~OBLIVIOUS~
THE WITHER IS BACK. DON'T ASK ME HOW, BUT ATRIA AND I JUST SAW IT. IT FLEW OFF.
YOU'RE KIDDING.
I WOULDN'T JOKE ABOUT SOMETHING LIKE THAT.
THAT LIAR! IT TOLD ME IT WANTED TO BE WITH ITS FRIENDS IN THE NETHER WORLD!
Betrayed
SHOULD WE TRACK IT DOWN? WILKIE CAN FOLLOW THE WITHER ROSE TRAIL AGAIN—
...
whine.....
MAYBE IT WAS A DIFFERENT WITHER.
THIS WAS THE WITHER THAT JUST KICKED OUR BUTTS.

LOW MORALE
SO, WHAT ARE WE GOING TO DO?
WE'VE BEEN HIKING TOWARD WHITESTONE CITY FOR A FEW DAYS NOW. WE'RE CLOSE ENOUGH. WHATEVER WE DECIDE, WE SHOULD STILL HEAD THERE AND UPGRADE OUR ARMOR AND WEAPONRY FIRST.
YES! I NEED A NEW DIAMOND SWORD. BUT FIRST I'LL NEED SOME DIAMONDS.
ANYONE?
FRESH OUT.
GET YOUR OWN DIAMONDS!
ATRIA?
UHH, I'M USING MINE.
I STILL HAVE A HOSTILE MOB LURE CURSE, REMEMBER?
MY SORCERER NEMESIS LIVES IN WHITESTONE CITY.
ASSUMING SHE DOESN'T CAST ME TO THE NETHER WORLD ON THE SPOT, SHE'S YOUR BEST BET FOR THAT CURSE.

THOUGH IT PAINS ME TO ASK HER FOR HELP...
ORION! GIMME YOUR DIAMONDS!
WHO SAYS I HAVE ANY?
CRACKLE
A... BLAZE?!
THAT SHOULDN'T BE IN THE OVERWORLD.

VICTORY!
POOF
SPLASH
tremble
tremble
AHHHH
SPLASH
RUFF!
SIZZ
YOINK
YOU'RE SAFE, LITTLE BEES.
BZZ BZZ
I HOPE WHITESTONE CITY HAS THE LATEST FASHIONS IN WARRIOR CLOAKS.

LOOK! APPLES!
OOH!
FINALLY, SOME FOOD THAT WE DON'T HAVE TO HURT CUTE ANIMALS TO EAT!
YEAH, BUT APPLES AND PORKCHOPS GO **REALLY** WELL TOGETHER...
KIDS! LOOK!
THERE IT IS.

WHITESTONE CITY.
WHEN I GOT EATEN BY THAT WITHER, I THOUGHT I'D NEVER SEE THIS PLACE AGAIN.
THIS USED TO BE MY CITY.
Whitestone City <---
"We built this city with rocks and stones"
Lucasta
World's greatest sorcerer
500 feet --->
Trespassers will be fed to zombies
HM. I GUESS THAT'S HER HOUSE OVER THERE.
"WORLD'S GREATEST SORCERER"? MODEST AS USUAL.
SHE HAS ZOMBIES?!
shrug
IS IT... OKAY THAT WE'RE DROPPING IN UNANNOUNCED?

WHO DARES APPROACH MY--
YOU!
LUCASTA. DO YOU MIND IF WE PAY A SOCIAL CALL?
...!
I... GUESS NOT. COME IN.
PARDON THE CATS.
SKTCH

FEEL FREE TO DROP OFF YOUR EXCESS INVENTORY IN MY ARMORY OVER THERE.
IT'S VERY SECURE.
STAIRS FOR CATS?!
WHAT SORCERY IS **THIS?**
NO SORCERY, SENAN THE SIMPLE.
A DISCOVERY I MADE WHILE CONDUCTING MY EXPERIMENTS. I WAS ATTEMPTING TO BUILD A NEW AND FRIGHTFUL MOB GRINDER—
SPRING
WHEN, TO MY SURPRISE, I INVENTED THE CAT FOUNTAIN INSTEAD.
TRULY, THE MOST IMPORTANT DISCOVERY OF OUR AGE.
SO TELL ME, SENAN.
WHAT BRINGS YOU HERE?
WOW, SO MANY CATS...
ATRIA HERE HAS A CURSE ON HER.

IS ATRIA YOUR DAUGHTER?
WHAT? NO, NO!
SHE'S A FRIEND OF THE TWINS HERE, MY MONSTER-HUNTING APPRENTICES CAHIRA AND ORION. SHE'S A GOOD KID.
I'M HOPING THAT YOUR...
...EXPERTISE...
...COULD HELP US UNDERSTAND IT, AND MAYBE EVEN CURE IT. I'M NOT SURE HOW POWERFUL YOUR ENCHANTING IS ANYMORE--
IT'S STILL PLENTY POWERFUL!
THE NERVE! I'M SHOCKED THAT YOU EVEN HAVE THE GALL TO SHOW UP ON MY DOORSTEP.
WELL, WE WERE BATTLING YOUR WITHER AND SO I THOUGHT,
"HMM, I SHOULD PAY OLD LUCASTA A VISIT."
OH? I HAVE A WITHER? AND HOW, EXACTLY, IS IT MY WITHER??
THE TWINS AND I WERE PILLAGING A CERTAIN WOODLAND MANSION...
AH. YOU MEAN MY WOODLAND MANSION? THAT'S MY SUMMER HOME! I STOLE IT FROM THE ILLAGERS FAIR AND SQUARE--
SERVES YOU RIGHT!
THE WITHER-SPAWNING TRAP WENT OFF, AS I'M SURE YOU INTENDED--
ALL THAT WORK OF YOURS FOR NOTHING. YOU THINK I'D LEAVE MY GOOD ITEMS UNGUARDED LIKE THAT?
AFTER ALL THESE YEARS, YOU'RE STILL UNDERESTIMATING ME, SENAN THE SHIRKER.

DON'T CALL HIM THAT! SENAN NEVER RUNS FROM A FIGHT.
THAT'S SIMPLY HOW SENAN IS KNOWN IN THESE PARTS. YOU MIGHT BE TOO YOUNG TO KNOW THE ORIGIN STORY OF YOUR MENTOR HERE.
"BUT LONG AGO, WHEN SENAN AND I WERE YOUNG AND FOOLISH, WE'D HAD A SORT OF RIVALRY, RIGHT HERE IN WHITESTONE CITY.
{GLARE}
"HE AND I HAD ALWAYS FOUGHT HOSTILE MOBS AND KEPT THE CITY SAFE.
PULL
CHK
"MY MORE CREATIVE METHODS WERE NOT AS APPRECIATED BY THE FOLK OF WHITESTONE. SENAN'S BRUTE FORCE WON OVER THE CROWDS MORE THAN MY INGENIOUS INVENTIONS DID.
"AT THE TIME, THIS BOTHERED ME-- ALTHOUGH I ASSURE YOU I'VE GROWN OUT OF SUCH INSIGNIFICANT CARES AS POPULARITY.
Sand
CHEER
TRUDGE
SAND?! Whadda mess!

"I GUESS WHAT REALLY BOTHERED ME WAS THAT SENAN GOT BETTER TRADE RATES THAN ME, FOR HIS 'HEROISM.' I, MEANWHILE, WAS PAYING THE SAME RATE AS ANY FOOL WHO WANDERED INTO TOWN WITH AN EMERALD OR TWO."
CURSE YOU, SENAN.
I'M NOT GOING TO SAY NO TO AN AMAZING DEAL ON ARMOR JUST BECAUSE YOU'RE JEALOUS!
I'LL SHOW YOU ALL!
"SO I DECIDED TO PROVE, ONCE AND FOR ALL, THAT I WAS THE SUPERIOR CHAMPION OF WHITESTONE CITY.
"SENAN AND I HELD A MOB-FIGHTING CONTEST, RIGHT IN THE CITY SQUARE.
"I SET UP A DISPENSER LOADED WITH SPAWN EGGS, AND SHOCKED THE WORLD WITH MY PROWESS.
HSSS!
SPLASH
!!

"IT SHOULDN'T SURPRISE YOU TO LEARN THAT I WON. I WAS THE CHAMPION THAT DAY. SENAN SUCCUMBED TO THE HORDES OF MONSTERS, LOSING BADLY."
!
GO
SPONSORED BY WOODEN SHOVEL
POOF
HERE!
YOU GET HIS SWORD!
HIS PICKAXE!
YOU TAKE HIS SPIDERWEBS!
SPONSORED BY MINECRAFT DUNGEONS
TAKE IT ALL!
Be A Champion!
gasp!
"IT WAS THE KIND OF CRUSHING DEFEAT THAT NO ONE COMES BACK FROM.
"SO, SHIRKER THAT HE IS, SENAN RAN OFF, ASHAMED, HOPING THE SANDS OF TIME WOULD REMOVE THE STENCH OF FAILURE FROM HIS NAME."
punch
...I LEFT TO TRAIN! TO IMPROVE!

...THE CITY WAS LATER BESIEGED BY MONSTERS, AND SENAN WAS, OF COURSE, NOWHERE TO BE FOUND.
I TOOK CARE OF THE PROBLEM **MYSELF**, BUT FROM THAT DAY FORWARD, THOSE WHO SPOKE OF HIM, THOSE WHO BOTHERED TO REMEMBER HIM, CALLED HIM "SENAN THE SHIRKER."
I DON'T BELIEVE YOU!
YEAH! THAT'S NOT QUITE HOW *I* REMEMBER IT.
MAYBE AGE HAS MUDDLED YOUR MIND.
YOU JUST GAVE UP AND LEFT?
...MONSTER HUNTERS **NEVER** GIVE UP.
mrow
NEVER HERO WORSHIP, CAHIRA. IT'S A RECIPE FOR DISAPPOINTMENT, AS THE FOLK OF WHITESTONE CITY LEARNED ALL THOSE YEARS AGO.
...
NOW, LET ME SHOW YOU THE CROWN JEWEL OF MY MANSION--THE DUNGEONS!
YOU HAVE **DUNGEONS?**
I'M A MOB FARMER. I LIKE TO WORK FROM HOME, SO I'VE SET UP SOME DUNGEONS IN THE BASEMENT.
JUST THIS WAY.

ooohh!
IN THAT DARKENED CHAMBER, HOSTILE MOBS SPAWN INTO COURSING WATER THAT GUIDES THEM TO THEIR DOOM.
WARP!
ENDERMAN!
GET OUT OF MY HOUSE!
SPLSH
WARP
WHAT PESTS. ANYWAY, WHERE WAS I?
THIS ONE I CALL "THE CRUSHER."
LAVA MUST BE USED SPARINGLY, OR YOU RISK BURNING THE ITEMS THESE MONSTERS DROP.

I'M STILL PERFECTING MY LAVA PROCESS. I SHOULD ADJUST--
GRAH!
SLAM
huff huff
WHAT'S GOTTEN INTO THEM? THEY'RE SO ROWDY TODAY!
IT'S MY CURSE.
MONSTERS ARE INEXPLICABLY DRAWN TO ME, MORE THAN OTHER PEOPLE.
SO THAT'S YOUR CURSE? INTERESTING...VERY INTERESTING!
LUCASTA? WHY WOULD YOU WANT TO DO THIS ALL DAY? IT SEEMS... WRONG.
MOB GRINDING IS A VERY MISUNDERSTOOD FIELD. SOME HAVE SAID IT'S THE DOMAIN OF TWISTED MINDS.
BUT I CHOOSE TO IGNORE THE CRITICS AND FOLLOW MY PASSION. YOU KNOW WHAT THEY SAY--
DO WHAT YOU LOVE, AND YOU'LL NEVER WORK A DAY IN YOUR LIFE!
SO TRUE! ORION AND I LOVE FIGHTING MONSTERS; IT'S NOT EVEN WORK FOR US!

MAYBE WE CAN COME DOWN HERE AND TRAIN? WE CAN BE YOUR PERSONAL MOB GRINDERS--
ABSOLUTELY NOT! MY MACHINATIONS HAVE NO NEED FOR YOU.
YOU'D ONLY GET IN THE WAY.
HAH! WE'LL SEE.
YOU! CURSED ONE! COME SEE THIS DUNGEON. HERE YOU'LL WITNESS ANOTHER GIFT OF MOB GRINDING.
IT'S ATRIA...
KSHH!!
POOF
THE GIFT OF MUSIC!
A MUSIC FARM! IT'S...

IT'S BEAUTIFUL... YOUR VERY OWN MUSIC ROOM...
KSHHHH
hiss
CHK! CHK!
HRAHH
THE SOUND OF CREEPERS GETTING SHOT IN THE NEXT ROOM KILLS THE VIBE FOR ME PERSONALLY.
IT'S THE HOLY GRAIL OF AMBIENT HORROR SOUNDSCAPES!
DISC 11!
WARNING
heh
AH, OF COURSE! YOU'VE GOT CAT AS WELL. A TRUE CLASSIC!
CAT
original overworld cast
my Lab, my rules!
?
NO TOUCHING!
sigh

ATRIA, I'D LIKE TO STUDY YOUR CURSE IN ACTION. FROM WHAT I'VE SEEN SO FAR, IT LOOKS LIKE A VERY POWERFUL, BRILLIANT, BEAUTIFUL, TALENTED SORCERER PUT THIS CURSE ON YOU.
BUT TO FIND A CURE, I'LL FIRST NEED TO ANALYZE THE CURSE ITSELF.
IT'S REALLY QUITE PERFECT FOR YOU THAT I'VE GOT THESE DUNGEONS FULL OF MOBS. YOU'LL BE COMPLETELY SAFE AND COMFORTABLE--
I JUST NEED TO ADJUST A FEW FEATURES OF MY WATER LAVA ROOM.
DON'T TOUCH ANYTHING. THIS HOUSE IS BOOBY TRAPPED. IF YOU'RE SO FOOLISH AS TO TRY AND ROB ME--
JUST GO ALREADY.
I WANT TO STAY WITH THEM!
NONSENSE.
IN HERE. ATRIA.

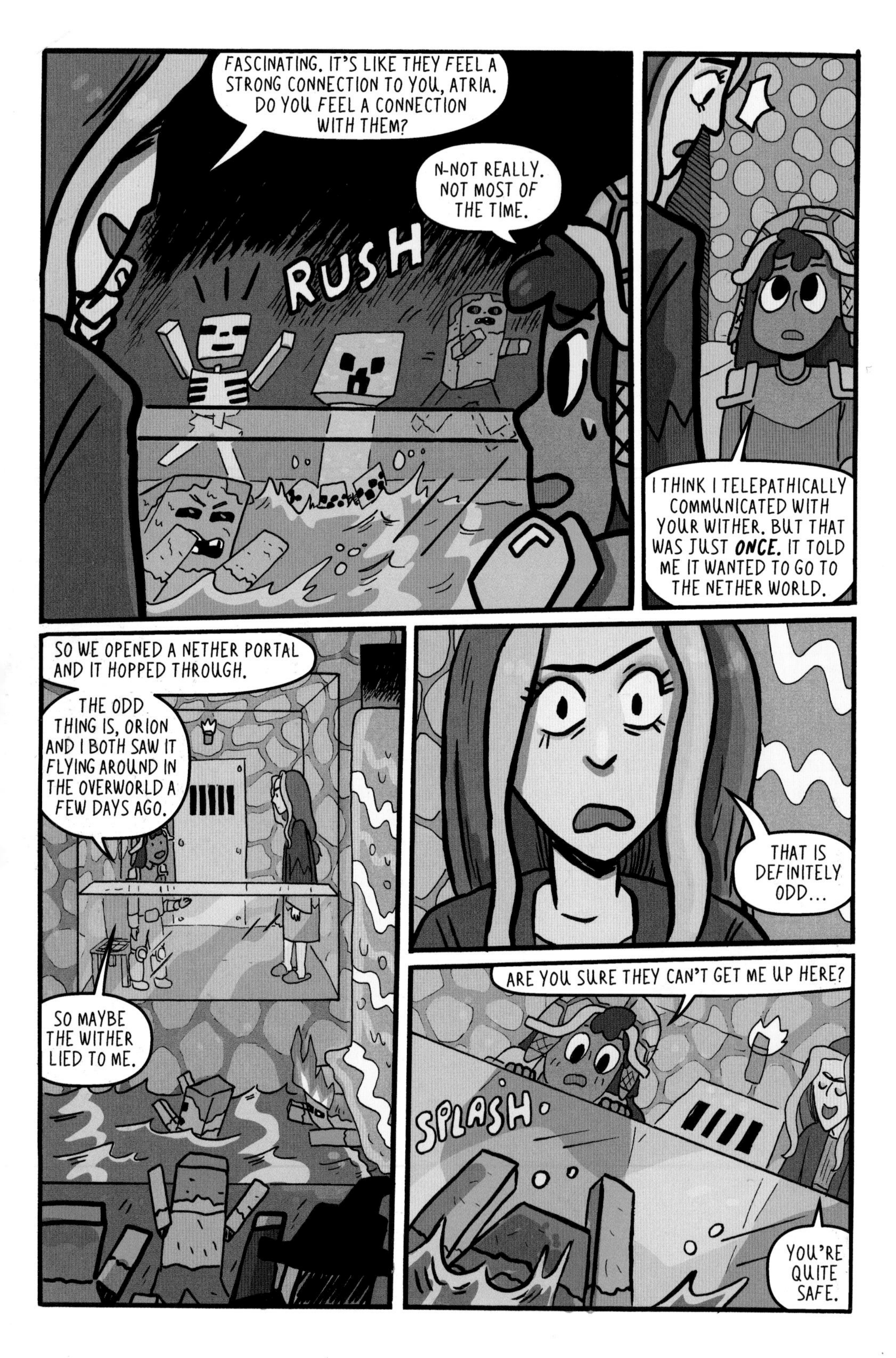
FASCINATING. IT'S LIKE THEY FEEL A STRONG CONNECTION TO YOU, ATRIA. DO YOU FEEL A CONNECTION WITH THEM?
N-NOT REALLY. NOT MOST OF THE TIME.
RUSH
I THINK I TELEPATHICALLY COMMUNICATED WITH YOUR WITHER. BUT THAT WAS JUST ONCE. IT TOLD ME IT WANTED TO GO TO THE NETHER WORLD.
SO WE OPENED A NETHER PORTAL AND IT HOPPED THROUGH.
THE ODD THING IS, ORION AND I BOTH SAW IT FLYING AROUND IN THE OVERWORLD A FEW DAYS AGO.
SO MAYBE THE WITHER LIED TO ME.
THAT IS DEFINITELY ODD...
ARE YOU SURE THEY CAN'T GET ME UP HERE?
SPLASH
YOU'RE QUITE SAFE.

JUST STAY ON THIS SIDE OF THE GLASS.
OKAY...
THIS CAMERA WILL ANALYZE YOUR CURSE. STAY PUT.
WHOA. CAMERAS ARE **REAL?**
IMPRESSIVE, NO?
YOU'RE LEAVING ME ALONE IN HERE?!
I'VE GOT TO CHECK ON THE OTHER DUNGEON CHAMBERS.
HUH. I DIDN'T REALIZE IT WAS POSSIBLE TO BE TERRIFIED AND BORED AT THE SAME TIME.

I DON'T GET WHY YOU THINK LUCASTA'S SO COOL. SHE REALLY ISN'T. SHE LOCKED ME INSIDE A MOB GRINDER ALL DAY. I DON'T THINK SHE WAS EVEN REALLY STUDYING MY CURSE.
ARGH, YOU'RE SO LUCKY, ATRIA!
ORION AND I WOULD HAVE SO MUCH FUN IN A MOB GRINDER ROOM.
THE DANGER! THE CHALLENGE! THE EXPERIENCE ORBS!
WE'D BECOME THE GREATEST MONSTER HUNTERS OF ALL TIME IF WE HAD A ROOM LIKE THAT TO TRAIN IN.
WOULDN'T WE, THOUGH?
BUT ISN'T IT ALL A BIT... GHOULISH?
I LOVE GHOULISH! GHOULS ARE COOL!
I WISH GHOULS WERE REAL.
UH...I FOR ONE AM GLAD THEY'RE NOT.
I JUST HAD AN AMAZING IDEA.
LET'S GO INTO THE DUNGEONS AND GET SOME LATE-NIGHT BATTLE PRACTICE.
BUT LUCASTA TOLD YOU NOT TO!

THAT FELT MORE LIKE A SUGGESTION, TO ME. PLUS, I REALLY WANT TO.
hehe
IF CAHIRA GOES, I'M GOING. I'M NOT GONNA LET HER BECOME A BETTER MONSTER HUNTER THAN ME!
ha!
HA HA! TOO LATE!
KNOCK YOURSELVES OUT. I'M GOING TO BED.
UNDER CONSTRUCTIC
NO ENTRY
HYAAA!!
SWSHH
KEEP IT DOWN WITH THE BATTLE CRIES!
OOPS!!
hy a a a...
HRRR!

YAWN I THINK IT'S MORNING ALREADY.
AGHH, TOO BAD OUR BEDS DON'T WORK IN DAYTIME...
YEAH, BUT IF WE STAY UP ANOTHER NIGHT...
WE CAN SEE PHANTOMS!
THEY ONLY SHOW UP WHEN YOU'RE REALLY SLEEP DEPRIVED...
I THOUGHT I HEARD THE CLANGING OF BATTLE! WHAT DID I EXPLICITLY TELL YOU? YOU'RE FORBIDDEN FROM THESE CHAMBERS!
BUT WE--
OUT! GET OUT!
Chastened
grr...

haha
ha
"Get OUTT..."
HI...
DID SHE CATCH YOU?
HAHA! YEAH! SHE WAS SO MAD!
IT WAS WORTH IT. I GOT GUNPOWDER, BOTTLES...
I EVEN GOT AN ENDER PEARL!
I GOT ROTTEN FLESH! SO MUCH ROTTEN FLESH!
THAT'S NICE.
WELL, IT'S BACK TO THE DAILY GRIND FOR ME. I BROUGHT SOME READING MATERIALS TO KEEP ME BUSY, AT LEAST.
ATRIA, DEAR! TIME FOR ME TO STUDY YOUR CUUUURSE!
SEE YOU LATER!
shuffle

ZOMBIE
Ingredients:
1 golden apple
1 splash potion of weakness
Time: 5m
My grandma always used this
recipe when we got bitten by zombies,
delicious!
What
SIGH
HRRR
DROP
mrow
I CAN'T BE IN THAT ROOM ANYMORE.
I'VE SPENT ENOUGH OF MY LIFE SITTING AROUND IN AN UNDERGROUND BUNKER SURROUNDED BY MONSTERS.
I HAVEN'T EVEN SEEN WHITESTONE CITY YET!
MEOW!
THAT'S IT! I'M GOING!
YOU COME UPSTAIRS WITH ME, LITTLE KITTY. IT'S DANGEROUS FOR YOU DOWN HERE IN THE DUNGEONS.

Some Enchanted ARMOR
EXCELLENT CHOICE WITH THE FROST WALKERS, SIR. AND AREN'T THESE PANTS JUST GREAT?
GRASSLAND FARMS GROCERY
FROST WALKERS
THEY'RE ENCHANTED WITH CURSE OF VANISHING, SO THEY'LL DISAPPEAR WHEN YOU DIE. THAT WAY NO ONE CAN STEAL YOUR PANTS!
THAT'S SO DUMB. WHY WOULD I CARE WHO HAS MY PANTS WHEN I'M DEAD?
THESE PANTS ARE ENCHANTED WITH THORNS--
STOP! THAT ONE'S ENCHANTED WITH CURSE OF BINDING.
YOU WON'T BE ABLE TO TAKE IT OFF.
HRRRM HRRM.
SHE SAYS, "YOU TRY IT, YOU BUY IT." NOW, WHAT KIND OF CLOAK ARE YOU LOOKING FOR?
OH, MY LAST CLOAK GOT BURNED UP BY A BLAZE, SO HOPEFULLY SOMETHING THAT CAN WITHSTAND SOME HEAT.
...SOMETHING THAT SCREAMS, "I'M ME, HERE I AM."
SA ARMOR SHOPPE
ARMOR
SALE
wave
I LOOK SO COOL!
I WANT MORE CLOAKS! I WANT **ALL** THE CLOAKS!

SALE
HAH! LOOK AT THE TOURISTS!
WE'RE NOT INTERESTED.
YEAH. YOU PROBABLY DON'T WANT TO MESS WITH US.
Smirk
OH, YOU'RE TOUGH, AREN'T YOU?
LOOK AT THAT SWORD! IS THAT IRON? WHAT HAPPENED, IS YOUR WOODEN SWORD IN THE SHOP?
har har
IT'S TEMPORARY--! MY DIAMOND SWORD BROKE IN AN EPIC BATTLE!
DON'T LET HIM BAIT YOU, CAHIRA.
I GUESS EVERYONE CAN'T BE AS COOL AS **ME.**
HAVE YOU EVEN **USED** THIS SWORD? IT LOOKS COMPLETELY PRISTINE.

I'VE SLAIN COUNTLESS MONSTERS WITH THIS SWORD!
I'M ELVICKS, THE GREATEST TEEN MONSTER HUNTER IN WHITESTONE CITY!
Cheer!
PROBABLY NOT ANYMORE. NOT SINCE WE GOT HERE.
YEAH. WE'RE **PROFESSIONAL** MONSTER HUNTERS.
LOOK, THESE ARE MY SPOILS OF VICTORY FROM JUST LAST NIGHT.
ANYONE WANT SOME ROTTEN FLESH? IT'S STINKING UP MY INVENTORY.
HRR?
YES, PLEASE!
MRRR!
PLEASURE DOING BUSINESS WITH YOU!
NOW I CAN BUY MORE CLOAKS!
hmph

SALE
YOU CAN'T BEAT ME IN COMBAT!
I WOULDN'T FIGHT YOU ANYWAY. MONSTER HUNTERS HAVE A CODE.
YOU'RE JUST SCARED YOU'LL LOSE.
haaa!
UNLESS YOU TURN INTO A ZOMBIE OR SOMETHING, I'M NOT FIGHTING YOU.
TURN
SALE
?!
SHOW 2NITE THE VILLAGER PEOPLE
HYAA!!
GASP
SWISHHH
CRACK!
I CAN MEND IT WHEN I GO HOME.
SO WHAT? I DON'T EVEN CARE!
heh heh

HRRN! MUMBLE MUMBLE.
YEAH! YOU'RE RIGHT!
HUH?
I'M THE FASTEST SWIMMER IN ALL OF WHITESTONE CITY, TOO. YOU'RE NOT MORALLY OPPOSED TO A RACE, ARE YOU?
WHOEVER GETS ACROSS FLUSHING RIVER FIRST WINS.
grr...
I'VE GOT THIS ONE.
PULL
I FORGOT TO MENTION, I HAVE AN ENCHANTED SWIM CAP! HAHAHA!
GOOD FOR YOU.
BEGIN!
whoosh

TRY TO KEEP UP!
JUMP
SPLASH SPLASH
FREEZE
SPRINT
You're cheating!!
ha ha!!
CHEER
REMATCH! THIS DOESN'T COUNT! YOU CHEATED!
CLUCK

CHEER
!!
HRN!!
uncomfortable
SHOW OFF
DON'T GET COLD FEET!
GET FROST WALKERS
• walk on water
• impress your friends
pat pat
THAT WAS SO SATISFYING! I'VE NEVER BEEN PROUDER TO BE YOUR SISTER.
...THE SWORD THAT CRACKED ELVICKS'S!
WELL, THAT'S OVER. YOU CAN...GO ON WITH YOUR DAY, EVERYONE.
FOLLOW~
THAT ELVICKS GUY WAS RIGHT ABOUT US BEING TOURISTS! SO, WHAT'S THE COOLEST SPOT HERE IN WHITESTONE CITY?

WOW...!
The Poisonous Potato AVANT-GASTRO PUB
FOUND THEM! YAY!
I DAIRY YOU TO MOOVE
MILK BAR
...ORION WAS BEING HIS USUAL SELF, LIKE, "THIS IS STUPID! WAHH!" BUT EVENTUALLY HE WENT ALONG WITH MY BRILLIANT PLAN!
SIGH
SO WE DIG A HOLE AND PUT A SPIDER IN HER HOUSE--I GOT BITTEN BY THE SPIDER SO MANY TIMES TRYING TO GET IT IN THE DANG HOLE--
ha ha ha ha
CAHIRA?
ATRIA!! COME MEET OUR NEW FRIENDS! ORION AND I ARE THE NEW CHAMPIONS OF THE CITY!
CHUK
WAIT!
I DIDN'T KNOW **YOU** PUT THAT SPIDER IN MY HOUSE.
so you heard that...

ATRIA!
I'M SICK OF BEING USED. BY LUCASTA WITH HER STUPID MOB GRINDERS. BY YOU.
I THOUGHT YOU WERE MY REAL FRIEND.
I AM! I REALLY AM! WE WOULD HAVE BEEN COMPLETELY LOST WITHOUT YOU, ATRIA.
SAVE IT, CAHIRA. FRIENDS DON'T MANIPULATE PEOPLE INTO DOING WHATEVER THEY WANT. AND THEN LAUGH AT THEM BEHIND THEIR BACKS.
BUT IF I HADN'T TRICKED YOU, YOU'D STILL BE IN YOUR LITTLE HILL, TERRIFIED OF MONSTERS--
JUST LEAVE ME ALONE. I DON'T WANT TO BE USED ANYMORE.
WAIT!!
ATRIA! YOU'RE, LIKE...MY BEST FRIEND! MY ONLY FRIEND, REALLY, 'CAUSE SIBLINGS, DOGS, AND OLD PEOPLE DON'T COUNT.
REAL FRIENDSHIP COMES FROM TREATING PEOPLE WITH RESPECT.
NOT FROM FORCING YOUR WILL ON EVERYONE, WITHOUT CARING ABOUT HURTING PEOPLE.
PEOPLE WON'T STICK AROUND IF YOU TREAT THEM LIKE...LIKE A BLOCK OF WOOD OR SOMETHING.
I GUESS I... DIDN'T REALLY LET YOU CHOOSE YOUR OWN PATH. I'D HATE IT IF SOMEONE DID THAT TO ME.
I WANTED TO GO WITH YOU WHEN YOU FIRST ASKED. I WAS JUST SCARED. BUT IT HURTS MY FEELINGS THAT OUR FRIENDSHIP STARTED WITH A LIE.
I'M SORRY...

I SHOULD GO BACK. LUCASTA'S PROBABLY LOOKING FOR ME.
I'LL COME WITH YOU.
WHAT--? ARE THEY JUST LEAVING WITHOUT ME?
WELL, UHH, THANKS FOR THE VICTORY MILK--
our first emerald
CHEER!
i need to get out of here
CHEER!
ORION!! ORION!!
BUT I'VE GOT TO GET GOING.
hrrrn...
Aww...
NO, NO, YOU DON'T NEED TO COME WITH ME. NICE TO MEET YOU. BYE.
hrn
?
GEEZ. I'M GLAD THAT'S OVER WITH. I FEEL LIKE I DRANK AN AWKWARD POTION.
sneak

MAYBE LUCASTA HASN'T NOTICED I'M MISSING.
I COULD GO SLAY SOME EXTRA MONSTERS IF YOU NEED TO JUKE YOUR MOB GRINDER STATS!
NAHH, THAT'S OKAY.
I CAN ALSO **NOT** SLAY MONSTERS!
CAMERA?
HI, LUCASTA!
TECHNICALLY I'M NOT BREAKING THE RULES BECAUSE I'M NOT ATTACKING YOUR HOSTILE MOBS.
ha ha ha
ha ha ha

...I'VE TURNED OVER A NEW LEAF! YOU'LL SEE! I'LL BE THE GREATEST FRIEND OF ALL TIME!
I'LL BE KNOWN THROUGHOUT THE LAND AS **CAHIRA THE PLATONIC!**
ha ha
WHAT ARE YOU DOING?!!
AAHH! LAVA!!!
FALL
AAHH!
CAHIRA!!
I'M FINE! SAVED BY MY TRUSTY FIREPROOF CLOAK!

CAHIRA! YOU SCARED ME!
WHY ARE YOU IN HERE, CAHIRA?! I EXPRESSLY FORBADE YOU FROM BEING IN THESE DUNGEONS!
yoink
THESE AREN'T FOR YOU!
whoosh
nods
CAHIRA WAS JUST KEEPING ME COMPANY! SHE WASN'T EVEN FIGHTING MONSTERS!
I...I BROUGHT YOU THESE, ATRIA.
?
I DON'T WANT THEM. I'M FED UP WITH BEING USED BY YOU TO GRIND YOUR PRECIOUS MOBS.
SIGH...
AH, YES. EVERYONE ALWAYS TURNS ON ME, EVENTUALLY.

hrrr...
MY BRILLIANT TRAPS AND MOB GRINDER PROTOTYPES NEVER IMPRESSED ANYONE IN WHITESTONE CITY.
VILLAGERS THOUGHT I WAS "CREEPY."
I CAN SEE THAT.
AND IT HURT WHEN SENAN CAME IN, AND WON THEM OVER SO EASILY.
WHEN WHAT HE WAS DOING REQUIRED SO LITTLE SKILL AND FORESIGHT.
JUST CHOPPING AWAY WITH A SWORD.
BABES STRAIGHT OUT OF THEIR SPAWN POINTS COULD DO IT.
HE WAS SUCH A SHOWBOAT, AND THEY LOVED IT.
WHEN I CHALLENGED HIM TO THE COMPETITION, WE AGREED THAT THE LOSER WOULD LEAVE WHITESTONE CITY FOREVER.
IT WAS WIN-WIN FOR ME, BECAUSE I NEVER FIT IN HERE ANYWAY, AND WOULDN'T HAVE MINDED A FRESH START.

BUT IN MY ZEAL TO WIN, I OVERLOADED THE DISPENSER WITH SPAWN EGGS. AND IT WAS GROWING DARK.
SOON THE CITY WAS OVERRUN WITH MONSTERS. IT WAS CHAOS. I EVENTUALLY CONFIGURED A POWERFUL ENCHANTMENT, AND BROUGHT THE VERY SUN BACK UP INTO THE SKY, SAVING THE CITY. BUT NO ONE CARED.
PTOO
AHHHH
/time set noon
THEY WERE JUST SAD TO HAVE LOST THEIR HERO. TO HAVE DISCOVERED THAT HE WASN'T REALLY **SENAN THE THOROUGH**, BUT RATHER, **SENAN THE SHIRKER.**
YOU **TOLD** SENAN TO LEAVE, THOUGH. WHICH YOU CONVENIENTLY DIDN'T MENTION BEFORE.
HOW IS HE A SHIRKER IF HE JUST FOLLOWED YOUR AGREEMENT?
WELL, IT'S NOT LIKE I TOLD THE VILLAGERS **THAT** PART.
BUT THEY NEVER TRUSTED ME ANYWAY. IT WAS THEN THAT I REALIZED I WAS WASTING MY TIME TRYING TO IMPRESS PEOPLE.
TIME I COULD HAVE SPENT AMASSING A FORTUNE IN MOB DROPS.
IF I HAD ONE REGRET, IT'S THAT I EVER TRIED TO WIN OVER THOSE FOOLS.

SO PARDON ME IF I WANT TO GRIND SOME MOBS. IT'S WHAT I DO. AND IF YOU'RE STAYING IN MY HOUSE, IT'S THE LEAST YOU CAN DO TO HELP ME WHILE I CONCOCT A CURE FOR YOUR CURSE.
WOW, LUCASTA.
SENAN! WH-WHEN DID YOU GET HERE?
hmm...
CURE
I HEARD ENOUGH, YOU LEGACY-STAINING CONNIVER.
THE OLD FARMER VILLAGER'S ALMANAC
"Highly recommended" —Librarian Villager
STAINING YOUR UNEARNED LEGACY IS THE ONE THING I DON'T REGRET.
GLARE

WOW, ATRIA... YOU'RE RIGHT. I'M SORRY. REGARDLESS OF THE SWANKY HOUSE AND COOL DUNGEONS... I NEVER WANT TO BE LIKE THAT.
"That"
Pat Pat
HUG
GEE, THANKS, CAHIRA.
NOT THAT I CARE WHAT ANYONE THINKS OF ME.
?
AHHH!!
WHAT WAS THAT?!
INTRUDERS!
THEY'RE IN THE ARMORY!
mow
?

YOU SAID THE ARMORY WAS SECURE!
!!
!!
!!
OUR STUFF! IT'S ALL GONE!
MY MAP'S GONE?!
YOUR MAP?
MY MAP TO MY HOMETOWN, WOODHAVEN! I DON'T KNOW THE WAY HOME WITHOUT IT!
YOU'RE FROM WOODHAVEN?
nods
NOOO
WELL...
...AT LEAST MY **SECURITY SYSTEM** DOESN'T DISAPPOINT ME.

YOUR MAP MIGHT NOT BE LOST JUST YET. FOLLOW ME.
STAND
I'VE BEEN BURGLARIZED IN THE PAST. SO I DEVISED AN INGENIOUS SECURITY SYSTEM.
IT'S A ZOMBIE SECURITY SYSTEM. IT FEEDS THIEVES TO MY HORDE OF ZOMBIES. THE ONES WHO TURN INTO ZOMBIES ARE FED INTO A MOB GRINDER.
THE ONES WHO DON'T... WELL...
THEIR INVENTORY IS GATHERED, INCLUDING WHATEVER THEY'VE TAKEN FROM US.
HARSH...
LET'S SEE IF WE CAUGHT THE THIEVES.
KRRR...
hrrn...

GRR...
ISN'T THAT... UH...THAT RUDE KID?
ELVICKS?!
HELP! PLEASE!
OH NO! IS THAT BABY ZOMBIE HIS LITTLE VILLAGER FRIEND?
AGHH!
YOU'VE GOT TO HELP HIM! PLEASE!
CHOMP!
PSYCHIC MOB POWER
HRRMm!
HE'S STILL IN THERE! I CAN TELL!
AND WHY SHOULD WE HELP THIEVES?
LUCASTA! THEY'RE JUST KIDS!

FINE!
PULL
BOTH OF YOU, THROUGH THAT DOOR.
OPEN
DASH
NONZOMBIE KID, GO TO THE RIGHT.
PULL
hrrr...
FWSH
CLANG

I--I JUST READ ABOUT A ZOMBIE VILLAGER CURE! WHAT WAS IT? AN APPLE-- UH...
I SAW THAT TOO! A SPLASH POTION OF WEAKNESS, AND A GOLDEN APPLE!
...A CURE?
LET'S GO!
yeah!
STAY PUT! WE'LL BE RIGHT BACK!
HEY! YOU'D BETTER NOT USE **MY** POTIONS!
YOU'RE GOING TO BE OKAY. THEY'RE GOING TO HELP YOU.
GRRR!!
HRRAAHH...

POINK
AGH! WHAT NOW?!
PORT
NO!
hrrah...
NO! STAY HERE!
scamper
scamper
hrrn!
SCAMPER
!!

CHK
CHK
COME BACK!
SPRINT
LOOK
NO...
meow
HRAAHH

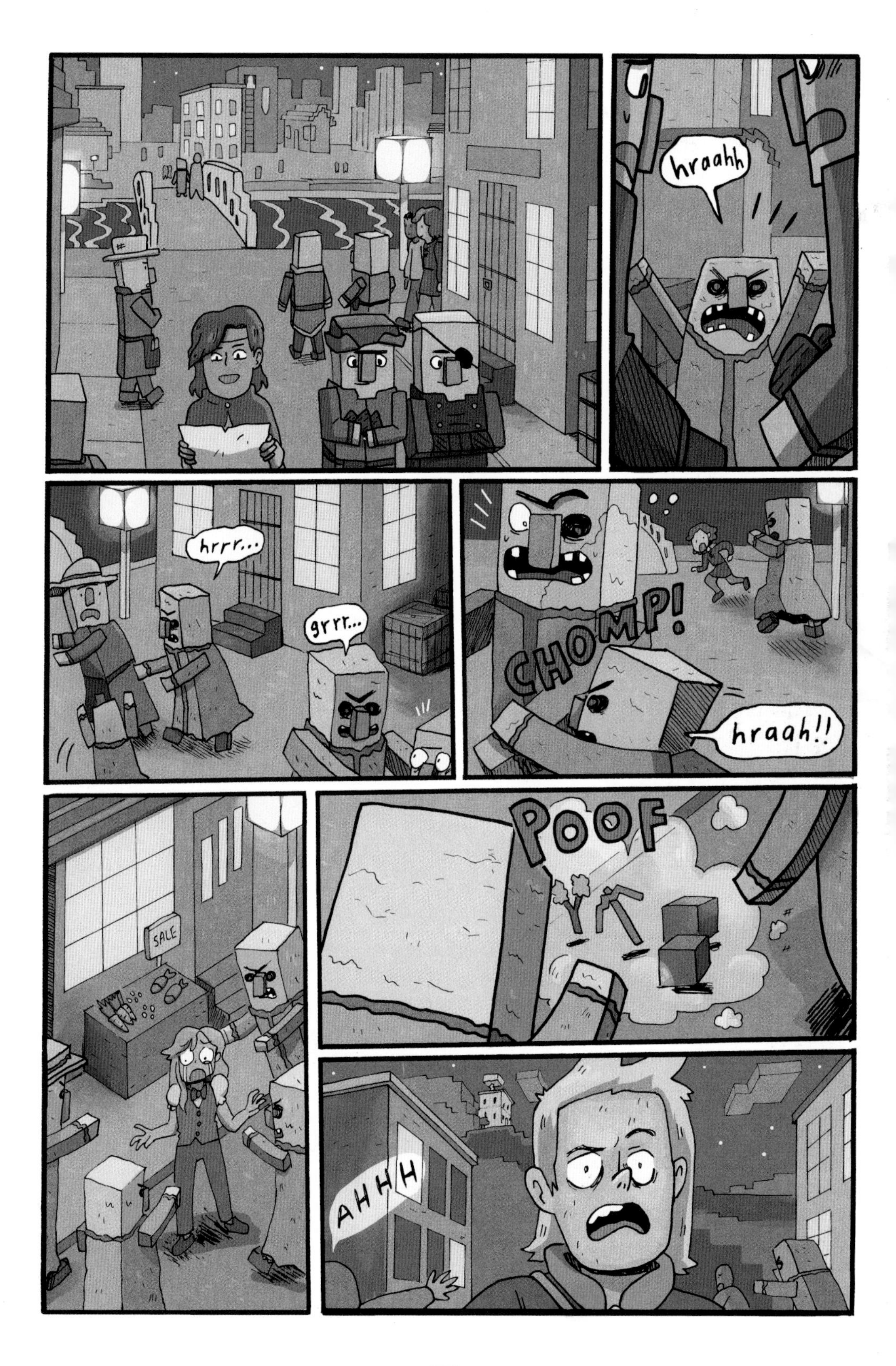
hraahh
hrrr...
grrr...
CHOMP!
hraah!!
SALE
POOF
AHHH

!!
NO! THERE'S A CURE!
PLEASE, WAIT!
JUST GET INSIDE AND LOCK YOUR DOORS!
hrr...
!!
AHHH
EVERYONE INSIDE! LOCK YOUR DOORS! ZOMBIES!!
RING RING

CLANG
CLANG
CLANG
??
OH NO...!
THEY GOT OUT?!
SHOULD WE GO FIGHT?
NO! WE HAVE TO CHANGE THEM BACK!
YOU'RE RIGHT... BUT DO WE HAVE ENOUGH SUPPLIES?
...
LUCASTA! DO YOU HAVE MORE POTIONS OF WEAKNESS IN YOUR DUNGEON?
I DO.
GO AHEAD, YOU KNOW WHERE THEY ARE.
SPRINT

I HAVE A WHOLE BUNCH OF APPLES!
ME TOO! WE JUST NEED--
...GOLD.
NO!!! NOT MY HOUSE! NOT MY GOLD!
LUCASTA, IT'S YOUR CHANCE. YOU CAN FINALLY BE THIS CITY'S CHAMPION.
...
I FORFEITED THAT A LONG TIME AGO.
BUT IF YOU SAVE THIS CITY... WHETHER THEY RECOGNIZE IT OR NOT, YOU'LL BE ITS TRUE CHAMPION.
ALL RIGHT. GO AHEAD, DISMANTLE MY HOUSE.
SIGH

CRAFT
my LAB my rules!
CLANG!
CLANG!

I'VE GOT ALL THE POTIONS OF WEAKNESS! EVERYONE, TAKE SOME!
CLANG CLANG
LUCASTA MADE A BUNCH OF GOLDEN APPLES!
EVERYONE, GRAB WHAT YOU CAN!
DROP
MY INVENTORY'S FULL!
MINE TOO!
LET'S GO!
JUST REMEMBER...
FIRST, WE SPLASH THEM WITH THE POTION! THEN GIVE THEM AN APPLE!
got it!
CLANG
CLANG
CLANG
!!

SPRINT
SPLASH
HRAAG...
FLING
DON'T YOU **DARE** BITE ME! TAKE THIS!
?!
FROS
WALKERS
?!!

SPLASH
HRR
CLANG
CLANG
hraah
LOOK! PHANTOMS!
WOW...
Hey!!! OW!!
!!
THEY NEED TO BE QUARANTINED FOR HALF A DAY, UNTIL THEY'RE FULLY CURED!
OTHERWISE THE ZOMBISM WILL KEEP SPREADING!
STAY STILL! GOOD ZOMBIE!
OKAY!

LAVA HOUSE
ESCAPE ROOM
tremble
hrr...
tremble
tremble
Ruff
Ruff
RUFF!
?
BARK
BARK!
HRNNN!
COSMETIC
SOLUTIONS
SKINCARE
Tired of
your face?
WE CAN HELP!
AFTER
WE SELL
SKINS!
This week:
25% off
Magma
Cream
RUN

CLANG
CLANG
THEY'RE TOO SPREAD OUT! WE DON'T HAVE TIME TO GET THEM ALL!
AND IT'S GOING TO BE MORNING SOON!
...!
I'VE GOT IT!
PLACE
hop
!
PLACE
COME HEEEERE, ZOMBIE VILLAGERS!
CLANG
CLANG
GOOD IDEA, ATRIA!
hrrr
hrr

CLANG
CLANG
THAT'S RIGHT, OVER HERE!
THE MOST DELICIOUS HUMAN IN THE OVERWORLD!
SPLSH!
Monch
??
HYAA!!
CUT THAT OUT! I'M HELPING YOU!

I WANT TO HELP! WHAT CAN I DO?
Oh! Uh...
TAKE THESE!
TOSS
AND THESE!
TOSS
...AND THIS DIRT! FOR BUILDING LITTLE SHELTERS AROUND THE ZOMBIES LIKE LUCASTA'S DOING!
x64
out of hands
QUICK! IT'S ALMOST DAWN!
TURN
CLIMB
DOWN

RGH!
?!
!!
SPLSH
THANKS!
OH
NO!
IT'S
MORNING!

WE NEED TO MAKE SURE EVERYONE IS PROTECTED FROM THE SUN! FOCUS ON PENNING THE ZOMBIE VILLAGERS IN!
AND TRY NOT TO GET BITTEN!
ISN'T THAT...
ELVICKS, ISN'T THAT YOUR LITTLE FRIEND?!
I'M OUT OF POTION! AGH!
ME TOO!
I'VE GOT ONE LEFT!
...BETTER NOT MISS!

Rgh!!
LOB!!
hrrah!
NO!!
DASH
HEY! ELVICKS'S FRIEND!
WHATEVER YOUR NAME IS!
TURN
?
Yagh!!
THROW

!!
DOUSE
YOU'RE OKAY!!
HRRN...
STAY BACK, KID. YOUR FRIEND IS UNDER QUARANTINE.
I GUESS HE STILL LOOKS... KINDA GREENISH.
CHK CHK
HEY, SORRY ABOUT EVERYTHING. AND SORRY WE STOLE YOUR STUFF.
WE OWE YOU OUR LIVES.
SHAKE
MAP

MY MAP!
MY ENDER PEARL!
MY SPIDER EYES!
sniff
Mew!
mew
Chomp chomp
AWW! LOOK, WILKIE MADE A FRIEND! HOW CUTE!
MEW!
YOU'RE SUCH A SWEETIE!
pet pet
HERE YOU GO, LITTLE KITTY!
TILT

munch munch
YOU WANT TO COME WITH US, LITTLE KITTY?
mew!
ELVICKS THE BRAVE RANG THE BELL AND SAVED SO MANY LIVES!
HRRN!!
HIP HIP HOORAY!
I'M THE ONE WHO SAVED THE CITY! THAT WAS MY GOLD YOU WERE EATING WHEN WE TURNED YOU BACK INTO VILLAGERS!
...AND I BUILT MANY OF THESE TINY DUNGEONS TO CONTAIN THE INFECTED VILLAGERS!
I SAW THE ZOMBIES COME FROM YOUR HOUSE!
yeah!
YOU STARTED THE WHOLE ZOMBIE OUTBREAK!
WELL, I TRIED TO HELP. ADIEU, FOOLS.
TURN
BY THE WAY, MAKE SURE TO LET THESE VILLAGERS OUT OF CONTAINMENT ONCE THEIR SKIN IS NO LONGER GREEN IN HUE.

WELL, WHAT ABOUT US? I THOUGHT WE WERE YOUR CHAMPIONS. WE CAN VOUCH FOR LUCASTA.
SOMEWHAT.
YOU'RE NOT OUR CHAMPIONS ANYMORE! WE LIKE ELVICKS THE BRAVE AGAIN! YAY!
?!
WOW.
WAIT! LUCASTA AND THESE TOURISTS REALLY DID SAVE THE CITY.
...TOURISTS?
I GREW UP IN THIS CITY! NONE OF THEM REMEMBER ME.
NONE OF THEM REMEMBER SENAN THE THOROUGH.
!!
NONE OF THEM REMEMBER SENAN THE THOROUGH...!
?
hrra!
THAT'S OKAY. WE THINK YOU'RE COOL.
YEAH!
THANKS, KIDS.
OH! CAHIRA, I MEANT TO GIVE YOU THIS.

I PICKED IT UP FROM THE ARMORER YESTERDAY. IT'S ENCHANTED WITH SMITE.
WOW!! I'M ENCHANTED WITH GRATITUDE!
USE IT WELL, KID.
AND I HAVE SOMETHING FOR YOU, ATRIA.
...I THOUGHT YOU LEFT!
THIS ENCHANTED APPLE SHOULD CURE YOU OF YOUR CURSE.
ALTHOUGH... IS IT ODD THAT I HOPE YOU DON'T USE IT? YOUR CURSE DOESN'T HAVE TO BE A CURSE.
NOT IF SHE TAKES UP THE MONSTER-HUNTING MANTLE AND STICKS WITH US!
THANK YOU, LUCASTA!
SO, WHERE TO NOW, SENAN?
NOT REALLY SURE. DO WE TRACK THE WITHER AGAIN?
...DO I NOT GET A PRESENT? I TAKE IT BACK, YOU'RE NOT COOL.

I...I THINK MY MOM IS PROBABLY REALLY WORRIED ABOUT ME.
NOW THAT I'VE GOT A CURE, MAYBE WE SHOULD HEAD BACK TO WOODHAVEN.
THAT SOUNDS LIKE A GOOD IDEA. AND IF WE FIND THE WITHER ALONG THE WAY...
...AND INSIDE HER HOUSE, SHE HAS A CAT FOUNTAIN!
DID I HEAR YOU MENTION MY CAT FOUNTAIN?
...IF WE HAD A CAT FOUNTAIN IN WHITESTONE CITY, WE'D BE THE HIPPEST PLACE IN THE BIOME!
I DON'T BELIEVE IT! THAT SOUNDS TOO AWESOME TO BE REAL.
I SHALL PROVE IT TO YOU!!
MILK
meow!
meow
MEW

HRAAAHH

EXTRAS

champion Discount

ATRIA OF ALL TRADES

THE FOUNTAIN

ART APPRECIATION

MINECRAFT™

SKETCHBOOK

CHARACTER DESIGN

Designs for Lucastra the Sorcerer...Lucastra has been Senan's rival since they were young and her favorite pastime was cursing him.

The (former and current) champion of Whitestone City, Elvicks and his best pal! Here we see the lil villager as normal and as a zombie!

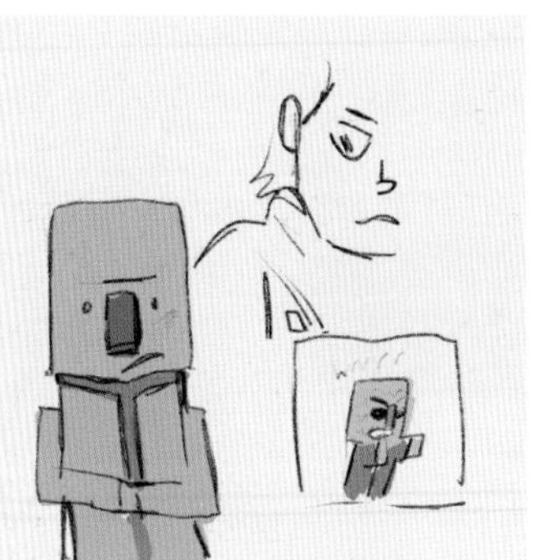

Cover sketches of Atria and the twins exploring Lucasta's dungeon, and Atria just hanging out in the mansion (what a view of Whitestone City!).

Cover sketches of Atria in Lucasta's mob grinder. It was fun to play with her reactions...in one version she is terrified of the mobs, in the other, well, it's just another day for her and her curse.

We went with this one. The approved cover sketch playing with Atria's reactions again!

Cover inks.

Kristen working on the *Wither Without You* volume 2 layouts.

Penny: "You're still working and not petting me?"
Kristen: "I'm almost done! I promise!"